WORLD OF STORIES

WORLD OF STORIES

SIX STORIES TOLD BY KATHARINE HEPBURN

ARTISTS

BRIAN LEE
THE MUSICIANS OF BREMEN
BEAUTY AND THE BEAST

GINNY HUMPHREYS
JACK AND THE BEANSTALK

ALISON CLAIRE DARKE
TATTERCOATS
THE NIGHTINGALE

CHRISTOPHER MARLOWE
THE EMPEROR'S NEW CLOTHES

HARPER & ROW, PUBLISHERS

For information address Harper & Row Junior Books,
10 East 53rd Street, New York, N.Y. 10022.

Printed in Singapore by Imago Production (F.E.) Ltd.

Library of Congress Catalog Card Number: 88-45076

ISBN 0-06-022296-4

First American Edition

Designed and produced by
Sheldrake Press Ltd.,
188 Cavendish Road,
London SW12 0DA,
Great Britain.

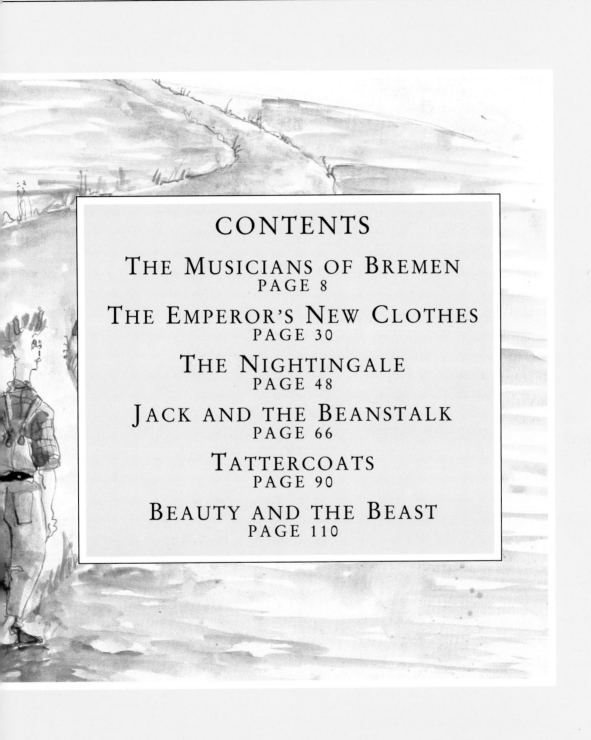

CONTENTS

FOREWORD

These stories are called fairy tales. They are the secret tales of the world of our childhood, when anything is possible. The animals talk, there are large beanstalks, people can be changed into animals. Anything – just anything – can happen. And of course, don't forget, virtue is its own reward. Help the weak. Do good. Punish the wicked. These are the messages that shine through the stories.

'Yes of course, Dad, we're old enough to catch on to that idea.'

But Gosh! Well, that takes me back a while.

When I was a child I listened, enchanted, as Grandfather Hepburn, who was a minister, told his special versions of fairy stories. He retold the old stories, but added something of his experiences and personality. And this is the way with the best of story-telling. It is live, it keeps on growing.

THE MUSICIANS OF BREMEN was his best. He could do it brilliantly. How I envied him! How I copied him! JACK AND THE BEAN-STALK also appealed to me very much. Oh! That beanstalk! If only I had a beanstalk in my garden . . . That is what is so great about fairy tales: you can think about them afterwards, and always think 'If only . . .', and away you go on a magic carpet.

My first acting part, at the age of 12, was the Beast in BEAUTY AND THE BEAST. I was the Beast with a sort of donkey's head. I wore blue velvet britches, vest and cape. They were trimmed with silver cord.

Ever since those early days I have loved stories and I think the only way to appreciate them is to act them or read them aloud.

So stories are for sharing, and it doesn't matter where you are in the world, it is the same: the story-teller and his audience, some who have heard it over and over but take comfort in what they know, others wide-eyed with wonder – the World of Stories.

THE MUSICIANS OF BREMEN

from

THE BROTHERS GRIMM

Now here's one you must listen to. My grandfather used to tell me this when I was a child.

Once there was a little donkey. He was very old and
very sad, because his master only gave him rotten
hay to eat, and he beat him often with a big stick.

"Old, worn-out, no more work left in you,"
growled his master.

"Oh dear!" said the donkey.

"I could sell your skin," said his master.

"Sell my skin?" said the donkey under his breath.

The donkey trembled. Then he whispered to himself, "Courage, Old Donkey. Don't give up, make a new life."

Next morning, just as the sun came up, he left his stable and he set out to find that new life. He had a pack on his back with all the possessions he had in the world, including his old spectacles.

The going was hard, and soon he was tired and he was lonely.

"Why couldn't I be a musician?" he puffed. "I could be a town musician, could I not, if only I could get to Bremen?" With this in his mind he managed to quicken his pace; one might even say that at times he was trotting.

After a while he met a dog, a very old dog, and a very sad dog.

The donkey put on his spectacles to look at him and said, "What's the matter with you, Dog?"

"I'm a hunting dog, but now I'm old and I'm slow and my master kicks me and beats me. I'm no use to him. What is to become of me? I am done for."

The donkey understood only too well. "Courage," said the donkey. "You come away with me. We'll make a new life. We'll go to Bremen to be town musicians. I can bray and you can bay. You can still bay, can't you?"

"O-O-O-OWE!" said the dog.

"How splendid," said the donkey. "Do that again, would you?"

"O-O-O-O-O-OWE!"

"Very nice," said the donkey, picking up his pack. "So off we go." And together they plodded down the road to Bremen.

After a bit they came to a cat sitting by a signpost, with a face as long as the road to Tipperary.

"Now then, Old Mouser, why so glum?" asked the donkey.

"You'd be glum too, if you were in my shoes," said the cat.

"Oh, I don't know," said the donkey. "If I'm not very much mistaken, in a manner of speaking, your shoes pinch, so your feet hurt, and when your feet hurt, you can't run.

"And if you can't run, you can't catch mice. And if you can't catch mice, well, you're no use to anyone. Isn't that about it?"

"He means you're old," said the dog.

"In a manner of speaking, that's about it," admitted the cat. "So what am I to do?"

"Well," said the donkey, "yours is a common problem."

"Admitted," said the cat.

"Courage!" said the donkey. "We're going to Bremen to be town musicians. Why don't you come along too?"

The cat perked up. "Me?" said the cat. "And will I be able to sing too?"

"Yes," said the donkey.

"At night," said the dog.

"Hop up on my back, Old Mouser," said the donkey, "and I'll give you a lift." And off they went together down the long road to Bremen. Each was happy in the others' company.

Presently a clamor filled the air: "Cock-a-doodle-doo!" They were passing a farmyard. There on the gatepost a cock was standing, crowing at the top of his lungs.

"Why are you crowing? It's afternoon, not morning," said the donkey.

"It's my last chance," replied the cock. "My mistress says she's going to chop off my head and make soup of me."

"Soup!" said the three travelers.

"Yes," said the cock. "So can you blame me? This may be my last song."

"Don't give up, Doodle-Doo," said the donkey. "Start a new life with us. We're going to Bremen."

"To be musicians," said the cat.

"But I've never been outside this farmyard," said the cock.

"Courage," said the donkey, "and you'll be alive tomorrow."

"Not much of a choice, have I?" said the cock, blinking his eye. "I'll be happy to join you. Cock-a-doodle-doo!"

"Good," said the donkey.

"Arresting," said the cat.

"Well, typical," concluded the dog.

Now there were four of them. They were happy and they made good progress. At last they stopped to rest in the shelter of a big tree.

Yes, it was pleasant, they all agreed, to be able to do what they wanted to do, when they wanted to do it, rather than being at the beck and call of a whistle or a whip or a "Here chick-chick-chick-chick-chick-chick!"

"No one ever called me," said the cat smugly.

"What about kitty-kitty-kitty-kitty-kitty?" grumbled the dog disparagingly.

It was dusk. "Take five," said the donkey. And they all lay down. The dog curled up and dreamt of juicy bones. The cat dozed, thinking of the saucers of cream she used to be given as a reward for catching mice. The cock thought of all the corn he'd been thrown and how the hens let him eat first. And the donkey tried a mouthful of grass, but it was poor stuff.

"No matter," he said to himself. "We're on our way to Bremen."

Then purely by habit the cock flew high up in the tree. "Look! Look!" he cried. "A light. A house in the woods!"

This might mean food. Up jumped the other three, and they all set off at once to examine the situation. They crept up to the house, they looked in at the window. There around a table sat three men. Obviously they were bad characters, and their table manners weren't good either. They were eating and drinking in a rude way, and boasting about the poor people they'd hit on the head and robbed of their money.

The four animals outside hit on a plan.

"Make a ladder."

Very quietly the dog jumped on the donkey, the cat jumped on the dog, and the cock flew up on the cat.

Then they all sang at the top of their voices. The donkey brayed, the dog bayed, the cat caterwauled, and the cock crowed.

"Ah-hee-hee! O-O-Owe! Miaow-ow-ow!
Cock-a-doodle-doo!"

Finally with a great push, they crashed open the
window and they burst into the room,
cock-a-doodling, baying, and caterwauling. The
robbers were terrified.

"What is it?" cried the first one.

"Evil spirits," screamed the second.

"Out!" yelled the third.

"I've gone," called the first.

And they all rushed for the door and at that very moment the door opened as if by magic, and they were helped on their way by a series of good swift kicks from our old friend the donkey.

"Our music has a great effect, has it not?" said the donkey, entering the house by the front door, as if it were indeed his very own.

Then the four musicians took their places at the table, and they ate and they ate and they ate.

But they did say "please" and "thank you" and "would you be so kind as to pass that bone?" The candle burnt low.

At last they could eat no more.

"And now to sleep," said the donkey, stretching. "It's been a long day." The cat lay down by the fire. The dog nudged up beside the cat. The cock whispered, "Sleep well. I'll tell you when it's morning."

"Lovely," they all murmured.

"So far, so good," qualified the donkey.

In the safety of the wood, the robbers had gotten over their fright.

"Light's gone out in the house," said the first one.

"Don't think it was spirits after all," said the second.

"You go back and see," said the first. So number three crept back into the house.

Moving up to the fire to give himself a moment's warmth, there he made his first great mistake. He stepped on the cat's tail.

"Miaow-ow!"

As you may imagine, the cat's response was anything but friendly, and as her claws drew across his face, he jumped away only to find that he had made his second great mistake. He had landed on the dog's paw. The dog sprang up and he sank his teeth into the robber's leg.

And, as he crossed the yard, the donkey kicked him
a solid blow with his hind foot. And from the roof
the cock cried, "Pitch him up to me! Pitch him up
to me!"

Running to the wood as fast as he could, the robber
screamed, "A witch scratched my face with her
nails. A man cut my leg with a chopper. A giant
beat me with a club. And on the roof sat a judge
calling, 'Bring the rogue to me.'"

"No place for us," said the first one.

"No," said the second.

"Run!" cried the third. "Run!" And they did.

So our old friends were left in peace. They finally had their own home. They were safe. And, after all their problems and all their troubles, they were quite ready to settle for living happily ever after. They had proved, had they not, in deed and in fact, that they were the musicians of Bremen.

"Time to go to sleep," said the donkey.

"Cozy," said the cat.

"Content," said the dog.

"Who could ask for more?" said the rooster.

And after a long pause, "Alive," said the donkey.

Well, that about sums it up, does it not?

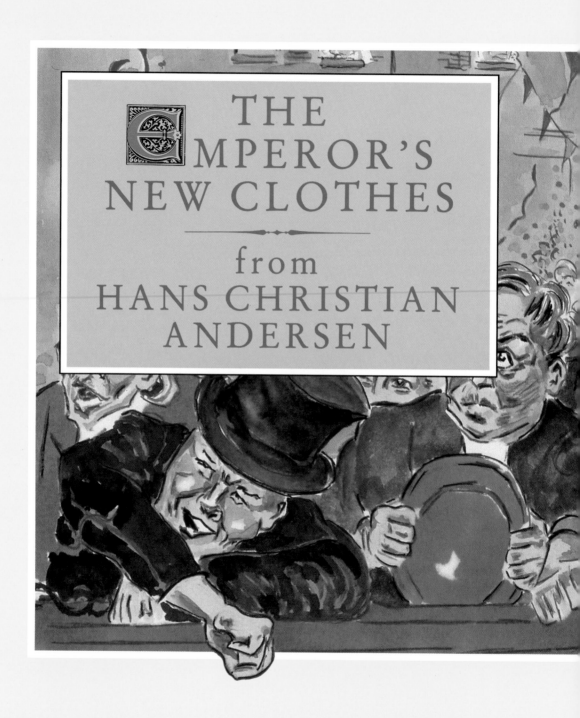

THE EMPEROR'S NEW CLOTHES

from
HANS CHRISTIAN ANDERSEN

ell, what do you think you would like tonight? The Emperor's New Clothes? I think you're going to enjoy this one.

A long time ago, there was an Emperor who was very rich, and he was very proud.

The Emperor, of course, was supposed to rule his Empire, but he left all the real work to his ministers and was totally absorbed with his own delicious silhouette. He simply walked up and down before the mirror in his splendid clothes.

Let's face it, the Emperor was very vain.

Now the Emperor was certainly the richest person in his country, and so naturally he could buy the most beautiful clothes.

They were made of silks and satins and velvets, and they were in lovely colors, too.

The Emperor looked at himself in his big mirror, and he murmured, not only to himself but to those nearby, "I am indeed, no question about it, the most handsome man that ever lived."

And everyone around him bowed and they said, "Yes, yes, of course, Your Imperial Majesty. Of course, of course."

Now the Emperor was willing to pay enormous sums of money for his clothes. Merchants came from far and wide with marvelous materials.

They came on camels, and they came with carts, and they came on horseback, and they came with packhorses.

They brought embroidered silk from China, glorious velvets from Venice, furs from Russia, anything from wherever, so long as it was the finest.

One day, two rogues heard about the money the Emperor spent on his clothes. "I wonder," said the tall, thin one to the round, fat one, "I wonder if we could cheat the Emperor."

"Why not?" said the fat one.

Next day they went to the great door of the palace. "Yes?" said the servant.

"We are very special weavers and tailors," lied the tall, thin one. "We weave magical cloth."

The servant laughed.

"You may laugh," said the tall man. "But our cloth is very special. Those who are stupid or not fit for their jobs can't even see it."

The servant felt a bit uncertain. "One moment," he said.

And the servant went to the Emperor, and he bowed and he said, "Most Gracious Imperial Majesty, there are two men here who say that they can weave the most extraordinary cloth. It can't be seen by anyone who is stupid or not fit for his job."

"Oh ho!" said the Emperor. Now here, he thought, would be a good test to find out which of his ministers and servants were worthy to be his ministers and his servants. "Let them in," he commanded.

So the two men, the tall, thin one and the short, fat one, were told to come in.

They climbed the stairs very slowly, as though carrying heavy goods. No one could see what they were carrying, but no one dared say so.

The two men went up to the Emperor. They bowed very low and then the tall one said, "Most Gracious Imperial Majesty, we have samples of our work."

And they held out their arms, and they seemed to spread out materials.

"Just look at this silk," said the tall, thin man.

"Just look at this satin," added the fat one. "Such colors. Soft as a butterfly's wing."

"Of course, Your Most Gracious Imperial Majesty," the tall one went on, suggesting the worst, "not everyone can appreciate them."

"No," said the fat one.

The Emperor nodded. He himself couldn't see anything, but he wouldn't say so. He certainly didn't want to be thought stupid and not fit to be Emperor.

So he said in a loud voice so that all could hear him, "I order you to make me the grandest, most beautiful suit of clothes that you have ever made."

"Delighted, Your Imperial Majesty," said the two men.

"Give them everything they want," commanded the Emperor.

"Oh, oh, Your Most Gracious Imperial Majesty," cried the fat one.

"You shall be well paid," said the Emperor, and a servant brought a bag of gold to the two men.

"Just . . . just one little thing. We shall need the very best silk and gold and silver threads to weave the cloth. And we need pearls and rubies to sew on the tunic."

And they came with the sacks of rich thread and the fine furs and the rubies and the pearls.

Every day the Emperor and his ministers and his servants came to see how the two men were getting on.

"Oh splendidly, splendidly, Your Most Gracious Imperial Majesty," said the tall one.

"Look for yourself," said the fat one, and he pointed to the loom.

Now, if everyone had been honest, they would have said they saw nothing, but such was not the case.

"Beautiful," said the Emperor.

"Magnificent," said the Chief Minister.

"Splendid," said the head servant, and everyone else agreed.

One day, the two men said that they had finished the cloth and must now measure the Emperor for his new suit of clothes. So they measured him, shoulder to waist, waist to knee, knee to ankle, shoulder to elbow, elbow to wrist, and they took his neck measurement and his chest measurement and his waist measurement.

Then, with their big scissors, they began to snip, snip, snip. "With precious cloth like this, we have to be very careful," said the tall one.

"Can't make mistakes," added the fat one.

And the Emperor and his ministers and his servants all agreed. But the Emperor was getting impatient. "I need my new clothes tomorrow," he said. "I shall walk through the town in procession. And I want my new clothes."

"Certainly, Your . . . Your Most Imperial Gracious Majesty," said the tall, thin one.

Next morning the two men said that they, and only they, could dress the Emperor. They carried, or seemed to carry, the new clothes to the imperial dressing-room. They helped, or seemed to help, the Emperor into his new shirt, his new tights, his new tunic, and his new cloak. And the Emperor looked at himself in the mirror.

"May I suggest the fur hat studded with pearls for this occasion?" said the tall, thin man.

Now the Emperor did not usually wear a hat. He liked to wear his imperial crown, then everyone could be sure that he was the Emperor and they would not take him for an ordinary person.

But, putty in the rogues' hands, the Emperor nodded and the tall, thin man placed, or seemed to place, a hat upon the Emperor's head.

"Oh! Oh! Your . . . Your Most Gracious Imperial Majesty!" cried the fat one.

"Marvelous," said the Emperor. "You shall be well paid."

"Such clothes!" "Such colors!" "Such style!" cried the ministers and the palace servants when the Emperor came into the great hall. Of course the news had spread about the Emperor's new clothes.

"Those who are stupid or unfit for their jobs cannot see them" had been whispered from one to another all through the empire.

Everyone had heard it. Even so, when the new young trumpeter saw the Emperor, his eyes nearly popped out of his head. "Odds bodkins!" he thought to himself. "Starkers!"

The great procession went down into the street: the trumpeters, the guards, the ministers, then the Emperor walking under a rich, embroidered canopy carried by four of the tallest African servants.

Everyone was there, in the streets, leaning out of the windows. "Hurrah!" they shouted. "Long live the Emperor!"

The two rogues thought that everyone would be so busy watching the procession that they were safe. They brought a cart to the side door of the palace. They loaded it with the sacks of rich thread, and fine pearls and furs and rubies, and being rogues they were trying to steal anything else they could lay their hands to. But no one noticed them. All eyes were on the procession.

"Oh, what splendid clothes!" cried the crowd. "What colors!" "What pearls!" "How well that tunic fits!" "Just look at that cloak!"

But one little girl who was right in the front of the crowd, pointed at the Emperor and said very loudly and very clearly, "He don't have no clothes on!"

The people around her went quiet. Then one whispered, "The child says the Emperor hasn't any clothes on." The whispers grew. "The child says, 'No clothes! Nothing on.'" "A little girl says, 'Naked! Naked!'"

The new trumpeter heard, the ministers and the servants heard. The soldiers heard. And so did the Emperor hear. No clothes! Could it be . . .?

"No clothes," someone in the crowd cried out at last, and everyone around him began to laugh. "No clothes!"

The young trumpeter spluttered and he turned his head away in a paroxysm of laughter. And there in the side street he spied the villains loading up the cart. "Thieves!" he cried. "Thieves! Stop! Thieves!"

"Charge!" ordered the General to his soldiers.

When the rogues saw the soldiers coming, they left all the riches and they ran for their lives.

But the crowd just stood screaming with laughter. It was hilarious. There had never been such a joke.

And the Emperor? Well, the Emperor. What could the Emperor do? Blushing scarlet from head to foot, he walked back to the palace as fast as ever an Emperor could, covered – or uncovered – only by his shame, or should we say only by his vanity?

THE NIGHTINGALE

from
HANS CHRISTIAN ANDERSEN

o you hear that? That is a nightingale. Now I'm going to tell you a story about a little Chinese nightingale.

Behold! The Emperor – the Emperor of China,
long, long ago. He was the most splendid Chinese
Emperor. And behold! He lived in the most
Chinese palace in the very heart of China.

The palace was splendid, too, and the gardens all
around were splendid and, of course, Chinese.
There were streams and bridges, flowers and trees,
all special to China. And can you imagine! Little
silver bells were hung in the trees, and when the
wind blew they tinkled prettily.

Far from the palace, way, way down in the heart of
the forest, lived a little bird.

She was a nightingale – a very special Chinese nightingale. Now this little bird had a very sweet song, and she loved to sing.

Travelers from faraway lands used to come to China, to see the splendid palace, and to admire the Emperor's great gardens. They listened to the pretty silver bells, and they were deeply impressed. But those who were really lucky heard the little nightingale sing.

"Oh! Oh! So beautiful!"

"It touches my heart."

And the little nightingale just went on singing her sweet song.

The travelers who had heard her said, "Of all the wonders in China, her song is indeed the most beautiful." Hearing this news, the Most Splendid Emperor called the Most Splendid Chief Adviser to him.

"We have heard," he said, "that certain travelers praise a nightingale's song above all else in China."

"Oh, indeed, Most Splendid Emperor," said the Chief Adviser, and he tried hard to look as if he knew what the Emperor was talking about. But in truth, he had never heard of the nightingale.

"Find it, and bring it here," commanded the Emperor.

The Chief Adviser questioned everyone in the palace, from courtier to cook. "A nightingale?" they asked. "And what might that be?" He asked here, he asked there. No one knew.

"The great palace gardens," he thought. And the first person he met there was a little kitchen maid.

"Girl," he said "have you heard of a nightingale?"

"Oh yes, Your Excellency," cried the little kitchen maid.

"Bring her to me," said the Most Splendid Chief Adviser.

"The nightingale lives in the forest, Sir," said the little maid. "Might I take the liberty of suggesting that you visit her in her own abode?"

Reluctantly, the Chief Adviser snapped, "You lead. I'll follow."

So they set off through the great gardens over the Chinese bridge, through a meadow toward the forest.

"Moo, moo," said a cow as they passed.

"The nightingale?" said the Most Splendid Chief Adviser.

"That's a cow," said the kitchen maid in amazement.

The cow simply watched them walk on. They came to the forest at last. There on a branch was the nightingale.

"There she is, My Lord," said the kitchen maid.

"That? The nightingale? Not much to look at, is she?" said the Most Splendid Chief Adviser.

"Wait until you hear her sing, Sir," said the little kitchen maid.

And before the words were out of her mouth, the little nightingale threw back her head, puffed out her breast, and from her throat . . .

"Wonder of wonders!" said the Chief Adviser. "Madam Nightingale, His Imperial Majesty would like to hear you sing. Would you be gracious enough to accompany me to the palace?"

"Oh," said the nightingale. "I'm shy. I sing best in the forest I know."

"But Madam Nightingale, the Emperor Himself..."

So she was persuaded and she went with him to the palace. Formalities concluded, the Most Splendid Emperor of China said, "Little Nightingale, we would like to hear you sing."

Without more ado the nightingale held herself very straight, she took a deep breath, and she sang. She imagined herself back in her forest, and she sang of all that she knew – of happiness and of sorrow.

The Most Splendid Emperor smiled, and then tears came into his eyes.

"Anything you want you can have," he said.

But the little nightingale said, "You have already rewarded me, Sir, with the tears in your eyes."

"We command you to stay forever in our palace," said the Emperor, and he had a golden cage made.

But the nightingale could not sing in a cage. So the Emperor let her out at least three times a day and said, "Sing, little bird." And thinking of her home in the forest, she would sing to the Emperor.

One day, the Most Splendid Emperor of China received a present from the Most Magnificent Emperor of Japan. "Not possible," murmured the Emperor as he opened the velvet-lined box. The Emperor of China – even this Most Splendid Emperor of China – had never seen anything like it.

It was a sparkling clockwork bird. It was a fantasy of diamonds, and sapphires, and rubies. Its wings were feathered in emeralds, and its bright gold beak could open and close.

"Begging your pardon, Majesty," said the messenger from Japan, clearing his throat with delight, "It sings." Then he wound up the glorious toy, and it sang.

"By all the great Chinese dragons," said the
Emperor. "It is beautiful." And he clapped his
hands. But no tears came to his eyes.

"Sing again, shining bird," he commanded. "And
you too, Nightingale," he added. "Sing together."

They did. The shining bird sang its few metallic phrases over and over again. The little nightingale in her modest attire poured forth her lovely tones, but her very soul cried out in despair.

And while the Emperor was watching the shining bird, and listening to its loud, hard song, the little nightingale simply flew out of the window, far over the great palace gardens to her home in the green forest.

In the palace the shining bird sang on. And every time it stopped the Emperor would wind it up again.

But one day, suddenly there was a whirring sound – the clockwork mechanism had worn out. Springs, nuts, bolts, and cogs fell on to the floor. The shining bird would never sing again.

The Emperor now, of course, missed the little nightingale. He realized his mistake, but he was too ashamed to ask her to return. So time passed. The Emperor was old, and he fell sick, and he felt sad, and as he lay there in his splendid Chinese bed, how he wished the little nightingale would sing to him again. But he realized that he did not deserve it. So the Most Splendid Chinese Emperor sighed. And he closed his eyes. And he folded his hands. He was giving up.

Silently into the room crept Death. The Emperor
heard him say: "Although you are the Most
Splendid Emperor of China, you will die."

The Emperor moaned. And with Death standing
before him, he felt indeed that he was dying.

Suddenly, as if in a dream, very softly, he heard the
most beautiful sound.

He opened his eyes, he looked up. And there on the
windowsill of the imperial bedroom was the little
nightingale. She had heard that the Emperor was ill,
and had come to give him courage.

She sang. She sang of hope, she sang of heartbreak.
And the Emperor listened, and he forgot his illness.
And Death listened.

And the nightingale flew closer to the Emperor, and she sang her heart out.

"Sing on," said the Emperor.

And the nightingale sang on, and with every note the Emperor grew stronger, and Death, of course, grew weaker.

Until, at last, the Most Splendid Emperor cried, "I am strong again. There is no place for you in my heart, Death." And, as simply as he had arrived, Death disappeared.

"Oh, thank you, little Nightingale," said the Emperor. And he got up, and he saw the sun on the blossoms, and he heard the wind in the trees and his tinkling bells, and he said, "I am well. I am alive."

The little nightingale flew off, back to the forest. But every day she came back to the splendid palace. Quietly, like a leaf, she flew in, and she sang to the Emperor.

The little nightingale sang with all her heart of happiness and sorrow. She gave courage to the Most Splendid Emperor of China. It was a secret between them. And always her beautiful song brought tears to his eyes.

JACK AND THE BEANSTALK

from
ENGLISH
FOLKLORE

Well, here we are again. Now let's see. Ready for an adventure?

Jack was a poor boy who lived with his widowed mother in a tumbledown cottage in the country.

Jack was, well, to be frank, he was lazy, and when his mother sent him to dig in the garden, he just leaned on his spade and dreamed.

So Jack's mother had to earn the living, and this she did by selling the milk from their good cow, Daisy-Bell.

One hot summer there had been no rain for months, and the grass had turned brown.

With little to eat, poor Daisy-Bell grew thinner and thinner, and her milk dried up. So Jack and his mother had no milk either, and they had no butter and no cheese to eat or to sell. So they, too, grew thinner and thinner.

One day Jack's mother said, "Jack, we must sell our good cow Daisy-Bell and we must buy food with the money. Take her to market and get a good price."

So Jack set off down the road with Daisy-Bell. He hadn't gone far when suddenly an old woman appeared in the middle of the road. Jack rubbed his eyes. Now where had she come from?

"Hello, my fine young man," said the old woman. "Where are you off to?"

"I'm going to market, ma'am, to sell Daisy-Bell."

"Sell your cow, eh? I hope you're good at buying and selling."

"Of course," said Jack

"Prove it," said the old woman. "How many beans make five?"

"Two in your left hand, two in your right, and one in your mouth, " said Jack.

"Right," croaked the old woman. "And there you are." And she held out five large but very funny-looking beans. "I'll give you these for the cow."

"Beans!" said Jack scornfully. "I want money and a good price, too."

"These are magic beans," said the old woman. "Better than any money you'll ever see."

Well, you remember Jack was a dreamer. So not knowing why, but somehow with confidence, he gave her Daisy-Bell and he took the beans.

"If you don't think they're magic by tomorrow, you can have your cow back," the old woman called after him.

And, without even a puff of smoke, she and Daisy-Bell disappeared.

So Jack went home. "How much did you get for the cow?" asked his mother.

"An old woman gave me five magic beans," said Jack. "And if they aren't magic we can have Daisy-Bell back tomorrow."

"You fool! And who is this old woman? And where does she live?"

Well, Jack didn't know, of course, and he began to think he hadn't been very clever after all. And as for his mother, she was so angry that she snatched the beans from his hand and she threw them out of the window.

But before you could say "knife," to the wonder of Jack and to the horror of his mother, one of the beans began to sprout. They couldn't believe their eyes. It grew, and it grew, and it grew. Up, up, up, an enormous beanstalk.

"It's magic," said Jack. "I'm going up."

"But you don't know where you're going," said his mother.

"That's the point," said Jack, as he disappeared into the green leaves of the enormous beanstalk. Then at last he came out into the brilliant sunlight above the clouds. He had arrived at the top of the beanstalk. He looked around.

"A pathway," said Jack. "I wonder where it goes," and immediately he set off to find out.

He came to an enormous castle. He knocked on the
door. The door opened and there stood a big, big
woman. "What do you want?"

"I'm hungry," yelled Jack.

"Look here, young man, this is no place for you.
My husband, the giant, could eat two like you for
dinner."

"But I'm a boy," shouted Jack.

"My giant loves boys for dinner," said the big, big
woman.

Now Jack was very frightened but he was also very
hungry. "Please," he said.

"All right," said the big, big woman, and she led the way into the kitchen, and she gave Jack a slice of bread as big as a door. He had only just started on it when the whole place began to shake.

"Quick! Hide in the oven."

There was a roar like a terrible thunderstorm, and into the kitchen came the giant. He stood in the middle of the room, and he sniffed and he sniffed and then he roared:
  "Fee-Fi-Fo-Fum!
  I smell the blood of an Englishman.
  Be he live or be he dead,
  I'll grind his bones to make my bread."

But his wife said, "Nonsense. Nonsense, lovey."
And she put a carcass of roasted beef as big as a
chair on the table before him. The giant ate it in
only a few gulps.

Then he got out his bags of gold to count. He
yawned and he counted, and he counted and he
yawned.

And then he fell fast asleep, and he snored.

Jack jumped out of the oven, picked up one of the bags of gold and ran off as fast as his legs would carry him.

Still a long way from the beanstalk, he heard a terrible roar. The giant was coming after him.

Then just when he thought he could run no further, Jack reached the beanstalk. Half climbing, half sliding, down he went until he was safe in his own garden.

"Oh Jack, oh my darling, darling boy," cried his mother.

But Jack said, "Look what I've got," and he showed her the gold. They were rich, or so it seemed.

But one day they found that they had spent all the gold. Should he go back to the giant's castle? Well, being Jack, he didn't hesitate.

And just as he got there, the door opened and there stood the big, big woman. "You again!" she shouted.

"Just visiting," said Jack. And again she let him in.

A few minutes later the whole place began to shake. Jack jumped into the oven and at the same moment into the kitchen came the giant roaring:

"Fee-Fi-Fo-Fum!
I smell the blood of an Englishman.
Be he live or be he dead,
I'll grind his bones to make my bread."

But the big, big woman only laughed at him.
"Come, come, lovey," and she put a bowl of stew as
big as a bathtub on the table.

The giant was hungry and he ate it in a moment. Then, yawning, he got out his magic harp.

"Play," he commanded it. And the harp played sweet music.

Of course Jack heard it, and Jack was enchanted, and Jack knew that he must have that harp. He waited. Soon, sure enough as was his habit, the giant fell into a deep sleep.

At the third snore, Jack jumped out of the oven. He seized the beautiful instrument and he made for the door. But the harp cried, "Master, Master," and the giant awoke.

Now the chase was really on. Jack ran as fast as he could, but a harp is an awkward thing to carry and the giant was only a little way behind.

At times Jack felt the giant's breath hot on the back of his neck. But he reached the beanstalk first. He jumped onto it, slid down, and was soon safely in his own garden.

Jack's mother was overjoyed to see her son safe again.

"Play," Jack commanded the harp, and it played the most beautiful music.

"Wonderful, wonderful!" said his mother.

But no one can live on music alone.

So for the third time Jack climbed the beanstalk. He walked up the path. He got to the castle. This time the door was ajar. The castle seemed empty. He slipped into the kitchen.

What was that? A noise like thunder. Jack leapt into the basket with the dirty clothes.

"Fee-Fi-Fo-Fum!
I smell the blood of an Englishman."

"I smell him too," roared his wife. She opened the oven. Jack wasn't there. They looked round the kitchen, he wasn't there; into the cupboards, he wasn't there; under the mat, behind the door, no, not there.

And the big, big woman put a pie as big as a bed on the table to comfort the giant. And he ate it. And then, feeling satisfied, he fetched his magic hen.

"Lay," he commanded, and the hen laid a golden egg.

Now Jack could see him this time, and his eyes nearly popped out of his head. A golden egg!

As before, the giant fell asleep. As before, Jack came out from his hiding place, moved stealthily across the room, seized the hen, and off he ran.

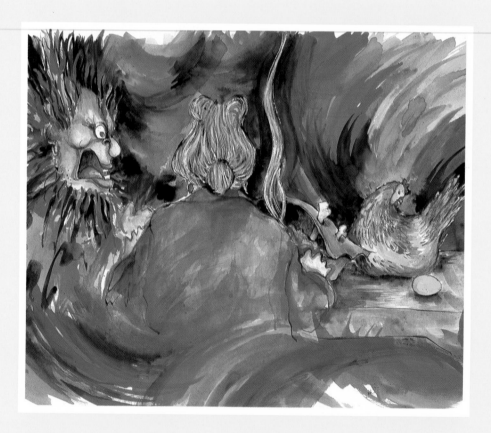

But the hen squawked and the giant awoke. Again the race was on.

Jack got to the beanstalk first, started down. But this time the giant was so mad he started down the beanstalk too.

It shook and it swayed with his weight, and Jack shouted as he slid down, "Mother! Mother! Fetch the axe! The axe!"

He took the axe from his mother, and with all his strength he struck that beanstalk with one wild, desperate stroke.

Down came the beanstalk, and the giant came with it. They fell so hard that the giant went right through the earth, and he disappeared, leaving only a huge hole in the ground.

Well, now we have come to the end of our story.

Just remember this, Jack was lazy. And from his point of view, it's too bad that he still has to chop up that beanstalk to get rid of it, and even worse that he has to use his spade to fill in the hole made by the giant.

But there is no doubt about it, Jack has a promising future. If you have a hen who can lay a golden egg when you say "lay," and if you have a harp which can play a magic tune when you say "play," you really do not have very much to worry about.

And you have learned that he who takes a chance has a chance.

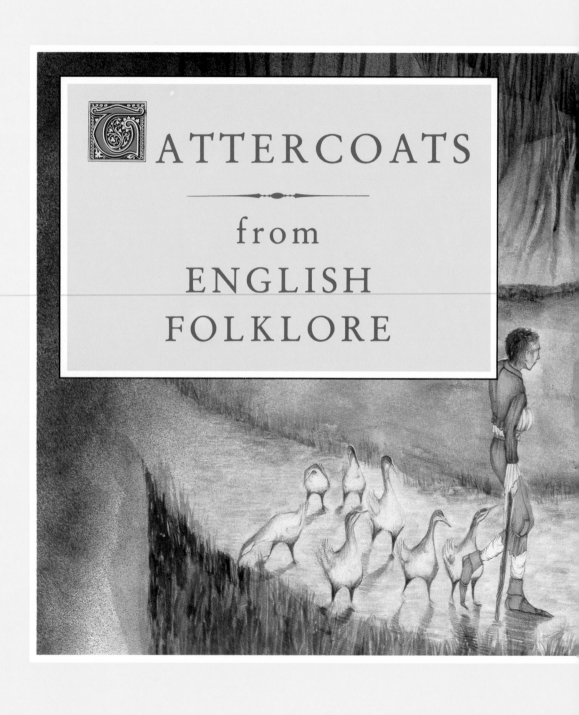

TATTERCOATS

from

ENGLISH FOLKLORE

Now here's a story I really enjoy. Tattercoats was a real princess. But she was poor, and she was often hungry, and she was often cold, and she lived in the dingy attic of a castle on the edge of the sea.

She was alone in the world, except for a faithful nurse who had always cared for her.

The great rooms of this lovely, old castle were occupied by her grandfather. You see, he was the King. But she never saw him.

He hated his granddaughter, and for this very sad reason: his daughter, whom he had loved more than life itself, had been married to a handsome prince. The prince had been killed in the Crusades. Shocked by the news, the daughter fell into despair, and the baby which she was expecting was suddenly born. The baby lived, but the mother died.

So the King blamed the baby. And he grew to hate
the very sight of her, and he made a vow never to
see her again. So great was his grief that he simply
sat alone, and he longed for death. Now, a sad king
makes a sad castle. And all the courtiers and the
attendants only saw the grim side of everything.

As a matter of fact, this is how the poor little
princess came by her name.

"Here comes Tattercoats," said an old courtier
spitefully one day as he caught sight of the little girl.

"True," she thought. "I am dressed in rags and tatters. But who cares? It's all I have." And she went on about her business.

Whenever the weather was fine Tattercoats would go out into the fields. There she had friends, a little lame gooseherd and his flock of nine geese.

The gooseherd told Tattercoats stories, wonderful stories of faraway lands, and he played lovely tunes on his pipe, tunes that sometimes made her heart ache, and sometimes made her laugh.

One day, a messenger arrived at the castle. He had
come from the King of the neighboring country
with an invitation to a great ball. And it was
planned that on this occasion the Prince would
choose his bride.

On the day of the great ball, feeling obliged to put
in an appearance, the old King dressed in all his
grandest clothes.

Tattercoats and her nurse looked out from their attic window.

"Oh, nurse," she cried. "How I'd love to go to that ball!"

But the old nurse shook her head slowly. "You know the King would never take you to the ball."

For a moment Tattercoats felt like crying. But she was by nature a happy person, so she went down the little back stairway, slipped out a side door, and was soon in the fields.

Tattercoats loved the fields. She could watch the sea crashing on the rocks below, she could see the gulls flying above. And there as always, at the edge of the largest field, were her dear friends, the lame gooseherd and his nine gray geese.

Tattercoats told them about the great ball. "Wouldn't it be fun?" she said, "just to see it all."

"Let's go," said the gooseherd.

Tattercoats stared at him. "But it's a long way."

"Yes, and I'm lame, and the geese have short legs, but we'll get to the palace. You'll see."

So the gooseherd played his pipe as he limped along. Tattercoats danced, and could it be that the geese did a sort of goose dance too?

The palace towers were in sight when a horseman rode up. Tattercoats smiled, the gooseherd played his happiest tune, and the geese honked.

"Where are you going?" asked the young man.

"We're going to the palace gates to watch the people going to the ball," said the gooseherd.

"May I walk with you?" said the young man.

"Of course," said Tattercoats. So the young man walked beside her.

"Have you any idea who I am?"

"No, no," replied Tattercoats.

But the young man smiled. "I am the Prince," he said quietly. "At the ball tonight I am supposed to choose my bride, because, as you know, a prince must always marry," and he looked a little sad as he spoke. Then he continued, "What is your name?"

"Oh, I'm, I'm just called Tattercoats," she said shyly.

"Tattercoats," murmured the Prince.

Now the gooseherd's music became suddenly strange and magical. The Prince looked down at her and she looked back at him, and the sound of the pipe held them spellbound.

The Prince blinked, then he smiled and said softly, "Tattercoats, you must come to the ball. Come at midnight. Come just as you are, and bring your good friend the gooseherd, and his nine splendid geese. Please, Tattercoats."

And the Prince mounted his horse and he rode off toward the palace.

Tattercoats stood quite still in the middle of the road. The gooseherd took his pipe from his mouth and he whispered softly, "Always seize your chance when it comes." And playing his pipe he limped off toward the palace, and of course Tattercoats and the nine gray geese followed him.

There were so many people around the palace gates that our little crew found it difficult to get near, but the gooseherd played his pipe and suddenly everyone let them through.

So Tattercoats, the gooseherd, and the geese stood by the palace gates, and they watched all the fine people arriving. They came in their newest and very best clothes. They came in ones and twos and threes, and with them came their footmen and coachmen, and their various attendants.

When the last of the guests had gone in, the onlookers lost interest and they went home. So Tattercoats and the gooseherd and his nine gray geese were the only ones left by the big palace gates.

They waited, and to pass the time the gooseherd played his pipe. Tattercoats thought she had never heard him play so beautifully.

When it was nearly twelve, the gooseherd changed to a new tune, and Tattercoats took a deep breath.

Slowly, just as the clock struck midnight, the gooseherd very solemnly said, "It is time," and they stepped into the great hall.

The musicians stopped playing; everyone stood still and stared. Never, never had these grand people seen anything like the little procession that walked slowly down the length of the great hall – a girl in rags and tatters, a lame gooseherd playing his pipe, and nine gray geese.

The King and Queen stared. Everyone else stared. Even the old King-Grandfather stared.

Then the Prince stepped forward, and he said, "Your Majesties, this is Tattercoats, and she is the girl I would like to marry – if she will have me."

The King and the Queen looked at the girl in rags before them. They had never seen a more beautiful girl. And Tattercoats looked back at them, and she smiled. And when Tattercoats smiled, it seemed as if the sun on a summer's morning was behind her eyes.

"My son," said the King. "Do you think that Tattercoats will agree to marry you?"

Tattercoats looked down at her rags and then up at the Prince.

"He wishes to marry you, not your clothes," said the Queen.

"And we would like you to be our daughter," said the King.

Tattercoats thought only for a moment. "I am honored of course, Your Majesties, and I am grateful to you, Your Highness," she added formally, giving the Prince a deep curtsey. "But I can marry you only if my grandfather thinks it a good idea." So saying, she turned to the sad, old King who was seated near her, and with an expression of such incredible love that it would indeed have melted the heart of a stone, "Please," said Tattercoats.

Slowly, with tears running down his face, the old King-Grandfather stood up.

"I think it's a very good idea," he said. "And why wait? We have wasted enough time, have we not, my beautiful grandchild?"

And the gooseherd played a haunting tune, and there was magic in it. And suddenly Tattercoats was standing by her Prince wearing a beautiful wedding dress, and behind her were nine page boys in gray-velvet tunics. And the musicians played, and the Prince and Tattercoats danced.

And the old King smiled, and the Prince and his parents smiled.

Then Tattercoats looked for her friend the little lame gooseherd. But he was nowhere to be seen. He seemed to have disappeared. No one could find him.

Then suddenly Tattercoats understood. "No need to hunt," she said quietly. "He is here – in our minds, in our hearts. He is always to be found in the smallest thing, the flowers, the fields, even in sadness – if only we look, if only we listen. He is our beauty, our happiness. He is our hope."

And suddenly everyone heard the haunting tune of the little lame gooseherd piping his way to another person who needed help.

BEAUTY AND THE BEAST

from
MADAME
DE VILLENEUVE

et me tell you a story, a story about a merchant and his favorite daughter.

The merchant lived in a big house with his three daughters. All were beautiful, but the two elder ones were vain and selfish.

The third was even more beautiful than either sister, and she was kind and loving. No wonder her father called her Beauty.

Then one day disaster struck. Three of the merchant's best ships were reported lost. He was ruined. And he had to take his family to live on a small farm which he owned in the country. Well, the elder girls just sat around complaining, while Beauty milked the cow, kneaded the bread, and swept the floors.

After some time, news came that one of the merchant's ships had been found.

"Thank God!" cried the two elder daughters together. "We'll be rich again. Father, bring us satin, brocade, silk, jewels, fine clothes, horses, a carriage."

"Yes," said the merchant. "And Beauty, what shall I bring to you?"

"Oh," she said carelessly. "Just a . . . well, yes, a blood-red rose."

"You shall have it," said the merchant. And he rode off.

But alas! Disappointment was waiting for him. The law claimed both ship and cargo. Months went by in legal argument. The merchant lost his case, and he was penniless.

And there was naught for him to do but to go home empty-handed, no presents for anyone.

By now it was winter and cold, and the journey seemed endless. He felt bogged down by dull despair. What would the future bring?

He rounded a corner and there before him was a gateway. The gates were open. Not thinking and certainly – certainly – not intending to trespass, the merchant entered the gate and went down the long drive.

At the end of the drive was a beautiful but small palace. The door of the palace stood open.

"Strange," thought the merchant.

He entered the palace. He called. No one answered. He entered the great hall and he called again. Still no answer.

"Albeit everything is set as if waiting for someone. For me?"

"Well, why not?" his conscience answered him. So he sat down, and he began to eat. The food was delicious, and the heat of the fire was a welcome change from the cold outside.

Feeling refreshed, he wandered about the gardens. Suddenly a beautiful rose caught his eye – a rose in winter.

"Ah, of course," he remembered. "I promised Beauty." So, without real thought, he picked the rose.

There was a sudden howl. And there stood a terrifying creature with a beast's head. And he put his hands around the merchant's throat. But they were not hands, they were paws with long claws.

The merchant was terrified, "Please, don't kill me," gasped the merchant.

"You steal my rose," said the Beast coldly. "Is that how you thank me for my hospitality?"

"I meant no harm. I promised a single rose to my daughter, Beauty."

The Beast growled but he took his claws away from the merchant's throat.

"Go," he said. "But in one week's time you must return here, and you must bring your daughter with you. If not, you will regret it." And with a strange moan he disappeared.

"I promise," began the merchant. But there was no one there to hear him. What was it? Who was it? A beast? A man? Who?

And before he could think further he found that he was home. Beauty was overjoyed to see her father again.

"My darling daughter," the merchant said, clasping her to him. And then, giving her the blood-red rose, he told her all that had happened in the palace of the Beast.

"We will return immediately," said Beauty.

So the next morning they were on their way. And the nearer they drew to the palace the more apprehensive they became.

As before, the gates were open, the door was open, the lights were on. They went in and they called, but no one answered. Finally, they ate the supper which obviously had been laid out for them, and it was indeed delicious. And then they went upstairs.

In one room on the dressing table was a beautiful blood-red rose, and beside it was a gold ring.

"The Beast seems thoughtful," Beauty mused. So the next morning, Beauty persuaded her father that he must go, and he must leave her alone in the palace with the Beast. Reluctantly, her father departed.

The Beast did not appear until the next evening. Suddenly in the flickering light he stood before her.

"Oh! Oh!" cried Beauty in amazement, and her heart seemed to stop beating.

The Beast spoke gently. "You have come to keep your father's promise. Are you not afraid?"

Beauty was too frightened to reply.

"I understand, of course. May I bid you good evening." And, so saying, the Beast disappeared. Next night the Beast came in again. And every evening it was the same. By degrees Beauty and the Beast found more and more to talk about.

Then one night the Beast said very simply, "Beauty, will you marry me?"

"Oh, Beast," said Beauty, her heart sinking. "I like you. I like you very much. But I could never marry you. No. Never."

And the Beast sighed, and he bowed his head in despair.

Evening followed evening. Always it was the same question. "Beauty, will you marry me?"

And always Beauty shook her head. "I cannot marry you," she said. She felt sorry for the poor Beast, but what was she to do? Then she thought of her father. "I wish that I could talk to him. Perhaps he could help me to find a solution."

She was standing before a mirror. And suddenly pictured there she saw her father. But he was alone and he was ill.

Her two sisters had simply abandoned him, and left him to fend for himself. Now she knew that she must see him. Beauty waited for evening. As usual, the Beast came into the great hall.

"Beast," said Beauty simply. "My father needs me."

"All right, Beauty, you shall go. Just place your ring on your pillow and wish. But be back before the end of the month – or I shall die."

"I promise, I promise, dear Beast."

And the next morning she found herself in her father's cottage. The old merchant almost fainted with joy when he saw her. So Beauty cared for her father, and she nursed him back to health.

Just before the month was up, her two sisters came to call. Bit by bit they heard her strange story. Then, with evil in their hearts, they plotted to keep her beyond the end of the month.

"Then the Beast will be angry and he will kill her," said the elder.

"And then we can share her jewels and her clothes."

To further their wicked scheme they said, "Our father needs you, Sister, only you."

And Beauty believed them, and she stayed on.

But somehow, somehow she kept worrying about the Beast. So again she stood before the mirror. "I wish," she murmured. "I wish . . ."

And in a flash, pictured in the mirror, she could see the garden, and there beneath the blood-red roses lay the Beast, as though dead.

"I must go," cried Beauty. And without more ado she took off her ring. She laid it on her pillow, and she said, "I wish to be with my Beast."

"Beast! Oh, Beast!" cried Beauty. "I've come back."

But the Beast lay motionless. "I am dying," he murmured. "Dying. You didn't come, and I know now that you will never love me."

"Oh, but I do," said Beauty. "I do love you. And I would like to marry you, and I would like to be with you all the days of my life."

And as gently as the fall of a rose petal, she put her arms around the ugly Beast, and she kissed him full on the mouth.

Suddenly, the Beast disappeared. And there instead was a handsome young man.

"Oh no, no. Beast, where are you?" she cried in despair.

"I am here," said the young man.

"No, no," said Beauty.

"Yes," said the young man. "I was under a cruel spell. It could only be broken if someone loved me, and promised that she would marry me."

So they stood in each other's arms, trembling with
wonder and with love.

Now we all know that people do not always get
what they deserve. But Beauty did. You see, she
had learned that fine presents can come wrapped in
brown paper. So with the Beast. He was so good, so
kind, so gentle of voice, so dear, in fact, that she
had quite forgotten that his exterior was not
conventionally acceptable.

"Oh Beast," for she would always call him thus, "is
this possible?"

"Quite," said the young man.

So they both sighed with delight, and . . . well, why
go on? They were married and they lived . . . ah,
you have guessed it. They lived happily ever after.